Sleepy
ABC

By MARGARET WISE BROWN

Pictures by
ESPHYR SLOBODKINA

HarperCollins*Publishers*

is for Aaaaah
when a small
kitten sighs

c is for Caw
when the
last crow crows

is for Dreams and the
Dark Wind
that blows

E is for Eyes that all must close—the child's, the rabbit's, and the rose

is for Feet that
won't fall asleep

is for Grazing
of sleepy sheep

H is
for Heaven
high
over head

is for me
who is going
to bed

J is for Jump,
and don't
bump your head

is for Kissing your mother goodnight

is for Listening
when they turn
out the light

M is for Mother
who tucks you in
tight

N is for the dark and starry Night

is for "Oh!" at
the story they read

P is for Pillow under your head

is for Quiet
that is all around

R is for Rabbits
that never make
a sound

S

is for Stars
that blaze
in the sky

T is for Time
that is
passing by

is for nothing
Under the bed

V is for Visions
that dance
in your head

W is for Work
you will do
the next day

X

is
for
all of the things
you can play

Y is for Yawning
before you sleep

Z is for Zipper.
Now zip into bed,
not another peep

GO TO SLEEP!